GENE LEBELL's

Grappling and Self-Defense For The Young Adult

Sketches by Bob Ryder

PRO-ACTION PUBLISHING
A Division of Pro-Action Sports, Inc.
P.O. Box 26657
Los Angeles, CA 90026

Originally published under the title, *Judo and Self-Defense for the Young Adult*. Republished by permission of Charles E. Tuttle Company, Inc.

Pro-Action Publishing A Division of Pro-Action Sports, Inc.
P.O. Box 26657, Los Angeles CA 90026.

Other books by Gene LeBell all from **Pro-Action Publishing**

- Grappling Master: Combat For Street Defense and Competition

- Gene LeBell's Grappling and Self-Defense For The Young Adult

- Gene LeBell's Handbook of Judo: A Step-by-Step Guide to Winning in Sport Judo

- Gene LeBell's Handbook of Self-Defense

Printed in the United States of America
ISBN # 0-9615126-5-2
Library of Congress Catalog Card Number 95-71804

TABLE OF CONTENTS

The sections following the Introduction, in rhyme and in illustrated step-by-step instructions, tell what to do when you are in the situations listed below.

⟨ 5 ⟩

INTRODUCTION

There once was a wrestler who thought
He was a poet so he went out and bought
A book full of words
About moonlight and birds
And deep philosophical rot.

He sweated and strained through the nights
Discussing the commonest fights.
He made it all rhyme,
At least most of the time,
And he reached educational heights.

His book, for protection, is good.
If studied with diligence it should
Help ward off a bum
Or discourage the scum
Who frequent the worst neighborhood.

I recommend this book to you all;
To the long, the short, and the tall,
For it tells how to beat
The bully or cheat
While having a lyrical ball.

This book was written for the untrained young adult who wants to learn how to "take care of himself" in those situations most likely to arise in his active, searching life—an attack by a bully, drunk, drug addict, or thief.

Simple, easy-to-follow text and pictures describe effective proven methods which can be learned quickly by almost anyone.

Hard-hitting, scientific blows, throws, locks, kicks, chokes, and disarming methods are carefully assembled in a concise handbook of selected methods which comprise the best of judo, jujitsu, wrestling, boxing, karate, aikido, savatte, and other "martial arts."

The rules of fair play were thrown out the window because this is a deadly serious little book designed to save you from a bad beating, or worse. Properly studied and applied, it will give you new confidence in your ability to stand up for your rights and defend your honor.

GENE LeBELL

TO UNDERSTAND IGNORANCE IS A STEP TOWARD KNOWLEDGE

1. If a man threatens to knock you to the floor,
   Don't make a scene, just walk him out the door.

2. Grab his wrist, pull him forward at his waist;
   He won't know what you're doing if you function with haste.

3. Drive his arm between his legs and grab his hair;
   Switch hands and walk him wherever you care.

4. Walk him outside impressing him that you are right.
   I'm sure he will tell you he doesn't want to fight.

1. If a man threatens you with an extended arm, take advantage of his weakness.
2. Grab his extended right wrist as though you were shaking hands. Pull it in close to your body and grab his belt with your left hand for assistance.
3. Shove his right arm between his legs with your right hand, grabbing his right wrist firmly with your left hand.

⟨ 10 ⟩

2

3

4

4. Grab the front of his hair, arching his head back,
and then walk him anywhere you please.

⟨ 12 ⟩

HOW YOU TREAT OTHERS IS HOW YOU GET YOUR TRADEMARK

1. Don't let a man squeeze you by the neck.
   If he does, you may end up a wreck.

2. Throw your hands up high in the air;
   Show him he'll get hurt if he doesn't play fair.

3. Chop his neck and give a shout;
   The shock of the strike will put him out.

4. Dust in his eyes will make them sore;
   A finger in the eye will hurt even more.

5. Stiffen your fingers and it will give you a longer
   reach;
   Jab toward his Adam's apple and he'll turn
   into a peach.

1

1. If a man grabs you by the throat, do something before he chokes you.
2. Place your hands together in front of your waist and, with momentum and force, swing them up

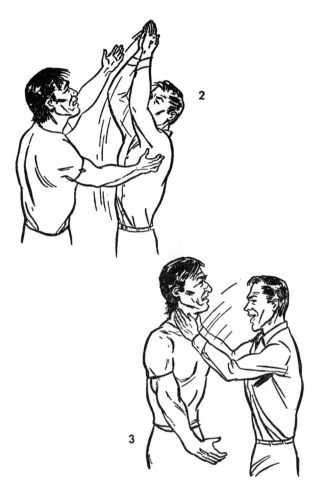

between his arms high over your head, breaking his grip.

3. Bring the blade side of your hands down firmly on the side of his neck toward the back.

4. If you ever get a piece of dirt in your eye, you know the pain can be excruciating. If a man attacks you, a slight jab in the eyes with your extended fingers will do the job.

5. Extend your hand by pointing your fingers, giving you a longer reach. Strike toward his Adam's apple instead of striking a hard surface like his forehead which might injure your fingers.

HAVING BRAINS AND MUSCLE DOES NOT MAKE THE MAN—IT'S HOW HE USES THEM

1. If a bully grabs you by the wrist, as this bully is doing here,
   And you know what you're doing, you will have nothing to fear.

2. Clamp his hand against your wrist so he can't get away.
   He'll quit when his wrist hurts, if you do what I say.

3. Put your free hand on his and lean toward the south.
   If you hear a scream, it will come from the bully's mouth.

4. If he has seen the light, forgive him and don't be mean;
   It doesn't pay to hold a grudge, so wipe the whole slate clean.

1. A man grabs your left hand, palm down.
2. Clamp his hand firmly against your wrist with your right hand.
3. Hold firmly and bend his hand until his thumb is pointed straight down.

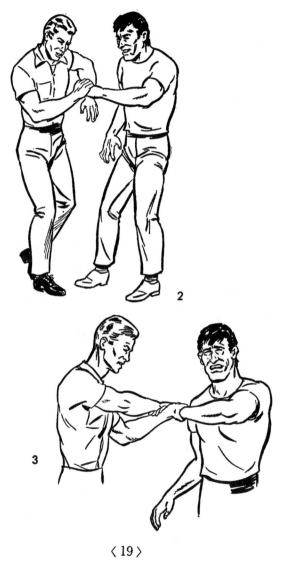

2

3

〈 19 〉

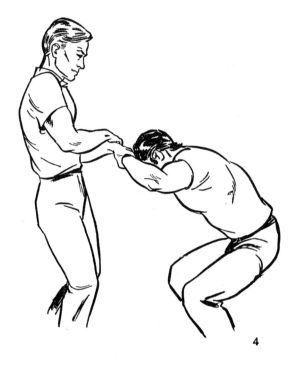

4

4. Press down with your left hand as you continue
   to hold his left hand against your wrist, forcing
   him toward his knees. (The pain is at his wrist on
   the little finger side.)

HE WHO WALKS WITH THE KNOWL-EDGE OF SELF-DEFENSE, NEVER WALKS ALONE

1. The bully grabbed me in a headlock, wanting to throw me to the ground.
   He walks up and down the street, saying he is the toughest around.

2. Quickly, I placed my left hand around his waist,
   Then placed my left leg in front of his with haste.

3. I raised my right leg as soon as my hip was in;
   He would fly through the air and that would rectify his sin.

4. Never brag about your talents or your winning charm.
   As you pat yourself on the back, you may break your arm.

1

1. Your opponent grabs you in a right side-headlock, putting pressure on your head and neck.
2. Place your left arm around his waist, pulling him near you. Then place your left leg in front of and below his knees in a lifting and tripping motion.

3. Place your right hand on his left wrist so he cannot get away, and straighten your right leg at the knee, thus raising him off the ground. Sweep your left leg backward, rolling him over the left side of your body and onto the ground.

〈 23 〉

4

4. After he gets thrown on the ground just once, he'll
think twice before grabbing a man in a side headlock again.

FAIR PLAY IS A FUN GAME AND CAN BE PLAYED ANYWHERE

1. He said my face was ugly and that he'd change it with a sock,
   But he faked me out and grabbed a left-handed side headlock.

2. I put my right hand under his nose and cover one eye.
   I place my left hand behind his left knee, around his thigh.

3. Lift at his knee and push his head back, using his nose.
   Off the ground in the air, he will take a vertical pose.

4. Land him on his back, he will be mighty sore;
   One thing is sure, he won't bother you any more.

5. Someone that can't produce anything else usually produces trouble,
   So know self-defense and burst his bubble.

1

1. If a man surprises and grabs you in a left side-headlock, escape before he does damage to your head and neck.

2. Place your left arm behind his knee in a lifting action and place your right hand under his nose, leaning his head backward.

3. Lift with your left arm at his left knee, shoving his head back by putting pressure on his nose with your right hand.

2

3

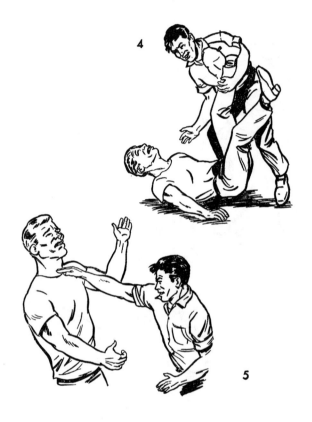

4. Hold his knee or leg high until he hits the ground.
5. If a man tries a side headlock on you, open your hand; it will give you a four-inch longer extension to your arm. Strike him at the Adam's apple and he will keep his distance. The best way to get out of a hold is to break it before it is secured.

HE WHO THINKS ONLY OF HIM-
SELF, THINKS WITH ONLY HALF
A BRAIN

1. The bully grabbed me from behind, he was
    going to give me a scare.
    I wrapped my right leg around his so he
    couldn't lift me in the air.

2. If I drove my right elbow into his gut,
    I knew I soon would be out of this rut.

3. I placed my right leg between his legs to get in
    the groove;
    I was turning from left to right and continuing
    my move.

4. I hooked my right leg behind his left leg, my
    palm lifts his chin,
    He will fall hard on his back; this is one fight
    he won't win.

1. If a bully grabs you from behind, do something quickly before he takes advantage of his position. Grapevine his right calf with your right leg so he cannot lift you high off the ground.

2

3

2. Spread your elbows apart to give you a little arm leeway, then strike the elbow at his solar plexus.
3. After you have struck him in the stomach with your elbow, place your right leg far between his legs.

4

4. Hook his left leg with your right calf. Then drive
your left palm up toward his chin. This will force
his head back and will send him falling to the
ground.

IF YOU LAY DOWN WITH DOGS, YOU'LL GET UP WITH FLEAS, SO CHOOSE FRIENDS WITH CARE

1. If he grabs you from behind and wants to start a fight,
   Break his hold; get behind him before he squeezes you tight.

2. Grab his wrist, spin to your left, grab his leg without fear,
   Lean down, lock his arm, pull his leg very near.

3. Pull his leg, until you're behind him, with vigor.
   Now you can handle him even if he is bigger.

4. Force him to fall past your right side,
   Then jump on his body for a winning ride.

1. This technique is called a switch-and-go-behind
   and is used when a man grabs you from behind.
2. Grab the back of your opponent's left hand with
   your right hand. Place your left arm over his
   triceps and grab between his legs, pulling his left

leg toward your body. Twist his left hand clock-
wise, with your right hand locking his elbow. Pull
your left arm in close and quickly step behind your
opponent.

3. Once behind your opponent, pull him very close.

4

4. Step slightly to the left side, placing your right foot
   at his right Achilles' tendon (back of ankle), tripping him backward over your right leg.

WHEN OPINION IS STRONG, OFTEN JUDGMENT IS WEAK

1. Here comes a bully looking for someone to test.
   He chooses our hero to show off who's the best.

2. My judo teacher said, "Don't ever start a fight,
   But if it should happen, know you are in the right."

3. I ducked under his right and tackled at his knees,
   He went on his back as pretty as you please.

4. I jumped on his body with my arms around his neck,
   My head was down low, my form I did check.

5. The bully sees I can hold him a minute, or all day.
   Says he, "I won't start fights, I'll be good—OK!"

1. If a bully comes down the street to test you, think before you make a move.
2. Your judo instructor will say, "Don't ever start a fight, but if it should happen, know that you're in the right."

3A

3B

3A. Like a football player, drive your shoulder and tackle at his knees.

3B. Lift at his knees until he is off the ground and he will fall sharply on his back.

4

5

4. Jump on top of him so he can't get up. Hook your legs around his and smother him slightly by putting your arms around his neck and hugging his upper body close to yours. (This will control the upper part of his body.)

5. Note that your legs are over his thighs and your feet hook him at the ankles, spreading his legs apart. (This will control the lower part of his body.)

TROUBLES MAY NOT MAKE A MAN RICH, BUT THEY SHOULD MAKE HIM WISE

1. He grabbed my lapel and told me he was the boss.
   I did not agree; to fix him would take one good toss.

2. So I grabbed his sleeve, twisted, and swung with my right;
   My arm around his neck, bending my legs, our bodies very tight.

3. I straighten my legs until he is off the floor.
   He will fly through the air while he's looking for the door.

4. Up and over my hip he goes with a great deal of haste.
   Move fast, know what you're doing, and there will be little waste.

5. Watch him sail through the air with the greatest of ease;
   But it is important to hold onto an arm so he'll land where you please.

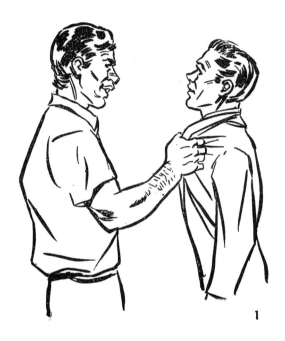

1. If a man grabs your lapel in a threatening motion, this is what to do.
2. Lock his right arm under your left armpit. Pull him in close with your left hand and start to wrap your right arm around his neck. Place your right foot near his right foot so that you can turn your back to him easily.

2

3

3. Your right arm is snug around your opponent's neck and he is pulled in very close to you. As you straighten your knees, you will note that this raises **him** off the ground.

4. Swing your body from left to right. As long as you keep your opponent in close to you, it will catapult him over your hip.

5. Continue to hold onto his arm or sleeve until he hits the ground. (This will protect your opponent so his head will not hit the ground, just his body. Also, you will have control of him, and if necessary can go into an advanced move.)

〈 44 〉

DON'T UNDERESTIMATE THE DEVIL; HE IS ALWAYS A TOUGH OPPONENT

1. If a man swings his fist to hit your shirt,
   Crouch, he will miss and you'll never get hurt.

2. Lean backward out of reach of his fist;
   Just bend at the waist with a backward list.

3. Clinch his left arm to your side if he wants to fight;
   Push your left at his biceps and he can't throw his right.

4. Clinch both his arms, duck your head, and look at your toes.
   He won't hurt you with his fist if he can't throw a blow.

1. The best way to defend yourself against an opponent is to be out of his reach. You will find it takes
much less effort to duck a punch than to block it,
so if a man swings a roundhouse left, bend at the
knees and his arm should fly over your head. But
just to be sure, raise your forearms up and cover
your temples, in case he swings too soon or you
duck too late.

2

2. If a rattlesnake strikes at you and the rattlesnake
   is three feet long and you are four feet away, he can
   strike all day and he will never hit you. The same
   is true of a man whose arm is three feet long. If he
   swings at you and you lean back four feet, he will
   miss you. In other words, stay out of reach.

⟨ 47 ⟩

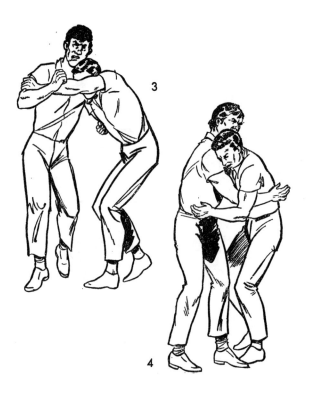

3. A man can't hurt you with his fist if he can't swing his arms, so one very good way to control his arms is to clinch with him. One type of clinch is when you wrap your right arm around his left elbow and hug it close to your body. Place your left palm at his right biceps in a pushing motion.

4. Place both of your arms over his arms, locking his elbows under your armpit. In this way, his arms are helpless.

CHEAT AND LOOK FOR A POINT-
ING FINGER; PLAY FAIR AND
LOOK FOR A PAT ON THE BACK

1. A boxer has little defense below his belt,
   So kick at the knee, it will really be felt.

2. Your leg is longer than your arm,
   So kick like a mule that lives on a farm.

3. Block his punch if he gets too near;
   Stay far enough away that your leg will clear.

4. Lean back, put your knee out at two o'clock,
   Flip your foot out, strike him with your sock

4

1. A boxer has little defense below his waist, so if you kick at his knee, it will be very hard to block.

2. Note, as you strike his knee, the upper part of your body is out of reach of his fist.

3. If he throws a roundhouse right, block it with your left forearm, staying far enough away from him so that you can strike or kick him with either leg.

2

3

〈 51 〉

4

4. Raise your knee and then quickly straighten out your foot. This will give you the opportunity to strike the man in the jaw easily with your foot and still keep your upper body out of reach of his striking hand.

DON'T GET A REPUTATION FOR BEING COMMON BECAUSE OF THE LACK OF COMMON SENSE

1. Controlling an opponent is important, I will tell,
   So I block his swing and grab his lapel.

2. Push his arm in front from your left to your right;
   His back will soon face you, you'll be out of sight.

3. Force your left arm up under his left armpit;
   When his lapel chokes his neck, he'll just have a fit.

4. Straighten both your arms at the elbows;
   Loosen your grip when he begins to doze.

1. Controlling an opponent who takes a swing at you is important. Block his right punch with your left forearm. Your right hand grabs his left lapel firmly.
2. Shove his right arm underneath and in front of your arm, spinning his back toward you.
3. Your right arm brings his lapel across his neck and your left arm goes under his armpit and on the back of his neck.

2

3

〈55〉

4

4. Straighten your left arm out. Pull with your right
   hand on his lapel. This will put a tourniquet on his
   neck. If you continue with this tourniquet action,
   you will cut the blood supply to his head and the
   man will pass out. As soon as he passes out, release the hold.

LOOK TO THE FUTURE; LIVING IN THE PAST IS NO FUN. NO MAN SEES HIS SHADOW IF HE FACES THE SUN

1. You start your flying scissors by stepping to his side;
   You lift his arm out of the way before you start your ride.

2. Jump in the air with a great deal of zest;
   Place a leg behind his knees, the other at his chest.

3. Use a scissoring motion and he'll spin like a top.
   (Practice this on a soft mat because it is a hard flop.)

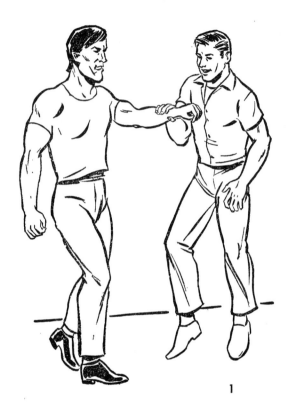

1

1. This is called the flying scissors. If a man extends
his left arm as though to push you, you'll find this
technique very valuable.

⟨ 58 ⟩

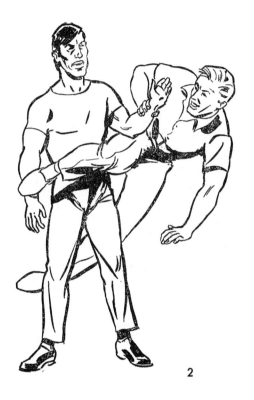

2

2. Hold your opponent's left wrist with your right
   hand. Jump at him, placing your right leg in front
   of his waist and chest. Your left leg is below and
   behind his knees.

⟨ 59 ⟩

3

3. Twist and spin your body sharply to your right.
   The momentum of your right leg against his chest
   will trip his body over your left leg at his knees.
   He will fall sharply to the ground and on his **back**.

IMPORTANT—START BRAIN BEFORE OPENING MOUTH

1. Please don't call me names in front of other guys.
   The only reason you do is the difference in our size.

2. He has got to get a lesson for giving me all that lip,
   And as his first lesson, I teach him a school-boy trip.

3. First, I grab him tight as I am doing here.
   The most important thing is to be very near.

4. You lean your body forward, this makes him lean back;
   You bring your leg around and drive with a whack.

5. Swing your leg up and boy he will fly.
   He will go down fast and only you'll know why.

6. So call me no more names or give me a line.
   Speech is human and silence is divine.

1. Name-calling is just one of the many ways a bully will start a fight.
2. If the bully has intentions of fighting you, get him before he gets you.
3. Grab your opponent, holding him very close. Wrap your right arm around his neck and secure

his left arm close to your side. Take a left step forward and lean forward. (This will make your opponent lean backward.)

4. With your right foot, trip your opponent by swinging your right leg between his.

5. Continue your sweeping motion between his legs, lifting him off the ground. Once he's off the ground, you may set him down gently or hard, as you will have control of his body.

6. With the knowledge of judo and self-defense, you'll find yourself a little taller in the eyes of a bully.

IT WAS CURIOSITY THAT KILLED THE CAT—NOT HARD WORK

1. You'll notice most fights that last, end up on the ground,
   So if the occasion arises, pin your man—this advice is sound.

2. Hold on tight, spread your legs apart;
   He won't be able to roll, not even start.

3. Hug his face to your chest so he can't breathe,
   Grapevine his legs, there is no way he can leave.

4. One arm hooks his leg, the other around his neck;
   Grasp your hands, duck your head, your form you should check.

5. Lift his lapels, rest your knee on his chest;
   The air will leave his lungs, he'll know who is best.
   (Learn to hold a man's body down so he can't get away.
   It might save you an embarrassing situation—tomorrow could be the day.)

〈 65 〉

1. Most fights end up on the ground, so if you can jump on your opponent and hold him down in some particular wrestling pin and control his body, this will end the fight.
2. Place your right arm over his right shoulder. Place your left arm underneath his armpit. Grab your hands together at the wrists and squeeze tightly.

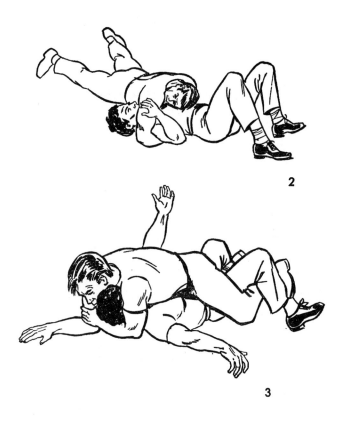

2

3

Duck your head and spread your legs in a tripod position for balance.

3. Wrap your left arm around your opponent's neck and over your right biceps. Squeeze his head close to you, smothering his face in your upper chest. Grapevine his legs to control his lower body.

4. Put your right hand between his legs and your left
   hand around the right side of his neck. Grab your
   left wrist with your right hand and squeeze tightly.
   Your opponent will find it difficult to move if
   there's a bend in his spine. (The more the spine or
   back is bent, the weaker your opponent will be.)

5. This technique is good in a situation where you do
   not want to get your clothes dirty. Grab your opponent's lapels—one in each hand. Put your knee
   into his short ribs. Lean your weight on your
   knee, shortening his breath, and pull firmly up on
   his lapels. (This is a good opportunity to control
   your opponent while you talk to him.)

TO GAIN SELF-CONFIDENCE, GAIN IN AN ABILITY IN WHICH YOU HAVE HAD NO CONFIDENCE

1. Running and jumping is a good way to get height;
   A good spring at your knees will make you feel light.

2. Strike as much of your body as you can when you hit land;
   Because if you land all your weight on just your arm, you might break a hand.

3. You break the shock by evenly distributing your weight.
   Hit your arms and legs at once, a safe fall will be your fate.

4. You won't get black and blue or in your head a hole,
   If you take time to learn a forward shoulder roll.

5. Roll a box down the street and the corners will break;
   Make yourself like a wheel and you'll roll like a snake.

1

1. A person learns to crawl before he learns to walk
   or run. When you start your tumbling, start rolling
   close to the ground, taking off from your knees
   before you start your take-off from a standing position or a running start. Then graduate to the
   standing role.
2. If you take a book and throw it down on its corner,
   it will bend or break. However, if you take the
   same book and slam it down just as hard on its
   flat surface, it will make a lot of noise, but there
   will be no damage done to the book. If you take

2

3

your body and, instead of landing on a side or a shoulder, hip or knee, land flat—it will give a chance for each part of your body to absorb its share of the shock.

3. Distribute your weight evenly instead of hitting your full impact on your head or hip. Land a pound on your arms, a pound on your shoulders, a pound on your back, a pound on your hips, a pound on your legs, etc. This way no one part of your body will absorb the full brunt of the fall.

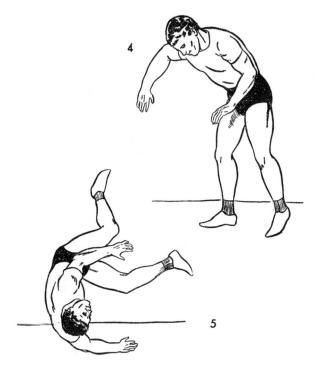

4. In rolling, make your body as much like a wheel as you can. If you roll a wheel down the street, nothing will happen. There will be a minimum amount of wear and tear. If you roll a cardboard box down the street, the edges will break and crumble, so when you roll your body make it as much like a wheel as possible. Round the corners so that you do not hit your elbows, shoulders, etc.

5. Continue to roll smoothly like a wheel, rounding off the sharp points of your body.

⟨ 72 ⟩

WHEN TWO RIDE THE SAME HORSE, ONE MUST SIT BEHIND

1. This is a girl.
   Her name is Pearl.

2. This guy has muscle, his hair is red.
   The muscle you can bet is all in his head.

3. He butts ahead in lines, he has to be first.
   Pearl goes into action with a burst.

4. She grabs both of his wrists, his actions she
   must stop.
   She will give him a lesson and swing him like a
   top.

5. Around and around he goes like a dart,
   And where he ends up is where he should start.

6. If a guy tries using muscle, strength, and force,
   Put him in his place, make him look like a
   horse.

2

1

1. Here is a young lady who likes justice and fair play.
2. Here is a boy who likes to take advantage of his size.
3. Here is a bully butting in front of smaller children because of his size.
4. Our heroine grabs the villain from behind at his wrists.

3

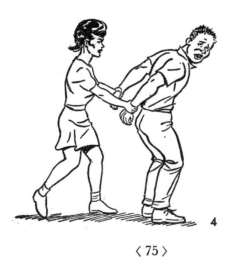

4

〈 75 〉

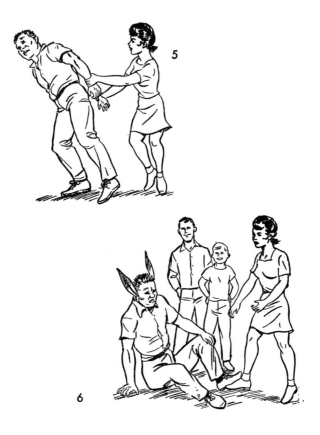

5. She swings him around, still holding him by his wrists. He will fly in any direction that she wishes when she lets go of his wrists.

6. When he falls down and ends up at the end of the line, he will look like anything but the bully who tried to butt in at the beginning of the line.

⟨ 76 ⟩

THIS MAN HAS AS MUCH GUILT AS A FOX IN A POULTRY YARD

1. I was watching a great movie in a comfortable chair;
   This joker put his hand on my knee, and that's not fair.

2. I grabbed his wrist and pulled his arm out straight.
   Girls, I wanted him to know that I was not his date.

3. Twist from right to left, drive your right wrist against his left forearm.
   Place his arm behind his back; it'll work like a charm.

4. When you do this move right, it is impossible to block.
   Grab his hair, pull it back, he'll be in a hammerlock.

1. If you are sitting down somewhere and a man comes and sits down next to you and puts his hand on your knee, you could be in serious trouble if you do not handle the situation quickly and with authority.
2. With your left hand, pull his arm toward your left knee, straightening out his arm.
3. Start to pull his wrist behind him. Make him lean forward by striking your right hand at his left elbow, rolling his elbow and body forward.

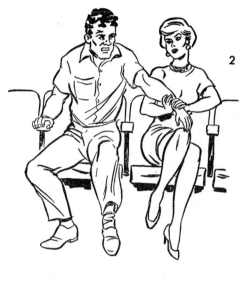

2

3

4

4. Place your right arm on his left biceps, raising his
left forearm up into a punishing armlock. So he
doesn't fall on his face, either grab the front of his
nose and pull it backward or grab his hair and pull
his head back. (This will put a great deal of pressure on his arm.)

EVERY GIRL KNOWS THAT THE BEST WAY TO KEEP A MAN AROUND IS TO KEEP PUTTING HIM OFF

1. He wanted me close so he grabbed me around the waist.
   He scared me even though I had to admire his taste.

2. He would not play fair,
   So I grabbed his hair.

3. My knee came up and struck him in the face.
   Shortly after, his stomach met my shoe-lace.

4. Be fair and just offer to take the young lady for a feed,
   And you'll make a friend, if a girl friend you ever need.

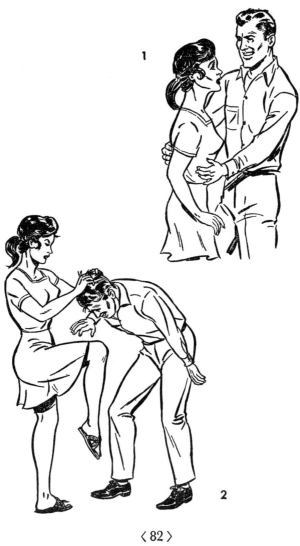

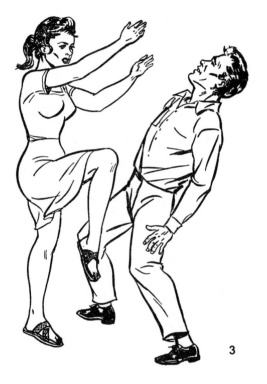

3

1. If you can't talk your way out of a masher's advance, react quickly.
2. Grab him by his hair and raise your knee sharply toward his face.
3. Raise your knee high and fast. The harder you strike, the more effective this technique will be.

4

4. A man is judged by how he treats others, so treat others as you would have them treat you—then everybody will be happy.

LOOK BEFORE YOU JUMP AT SOMETHING SWEET—YOU MAY END UP IN A JAM

1. This man jumped at this girl and hugged her
   and kissed her;
   It was easy to tell she was not his sister.

2. Her right hand threatened to give him a judo
   chop;
   His penalty for kissing was to take a flop.

3. Take a step to get closer, place your right leg
   behind his right,
   Grab his left hand, lean forward, and strike his
   shoulder with all your might.

4. Sweep your leg backward as hard as you dare;
   Follow through until he is in the air.

5. He will fly high in the air and land on the floor.
   He won't want to kiss you again, well, not
   while he's still sore.

1. If a man jumps at you to hug and kiss you, let him know that he cannot get away with it.
2. Strike at the bridge of his nose or his Adam's apple. He will let go quickly.

3. As he does let go, grab his right wrist with your
   left hand. Place your right leg behind his right
   knee. Strike your right hand at his right shoulder-
   blade as you lean forward.

4. Continue your forward motion, pushing on his right arm and, raising your left leg, lifting him off the ground.

5. Eventually he will land on his back. (It is worth the time to practice these techniques.)

FORBIDDEN FRUIT GIVES A SWEETER TASTE BUT WATCH OUT FOR A GREATER STOMACHACHE

1. He was in a car following me down the street.
   I could not run away with these two small feet.

2. He jumped out of his car, it gave me a fright.
   He grabbed onto my wrist and held on very tight.

3. I swung my body from right to left, and doubled up my left fist,
   And when I backhanded him, he wished I had missed.

4. He felt my backhand on the bridge of the nose.
   You know he felt it from his head to his toes.

5. Fools argue, wise men discuss.
   Learn self-defense, either way there will be no fuss.

1

1. If a man follows you down the street in a car, know where he is all the time so he will not be able to surprise you.
2. If he jumps out of the car and grabs you by the wrist, watch your balance so you do not fall to the ground.
3. Twist away from him, gaining momentum. Double up your free fist.

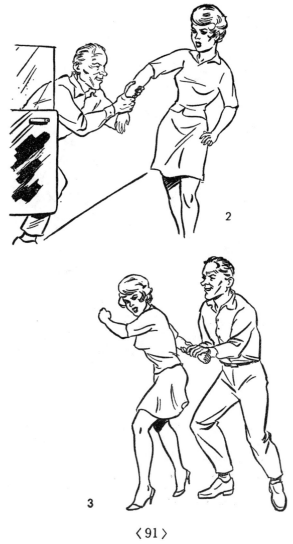

2

3

〈91〉

4

5

4. Swing your free fist back like a pendulum, striking the man on the bridge of his nose. This will make him let go fast as he drops to the ground.

5. If you step on him or kick him when he is down, this will let him know that not all women can be taken advantage of by a masher.

IF POVERTY IS THE MOTHER OF CRIME, THEN FOOLISHNESS IS THE FATHER

1. I saw a crook take an old lady's purse and run.
   I had to stop him until help could come.

2. I used my karate kick to knock him out of breath.
   He fell on his back and had nothing left.

3. I jumped on his body before he could get off his back;
   I grabbed his left arm and began my ground attack.

4. This hold-down is called a side pin, they say.
   Get anyone in this and you can hold him all day.

5. I put my right hand around his neck, spread my legs for a better stance.
   He will try in every way to get up, but has very little chance.

1

1. If you see somebody doing a wrong, try to right this wrong and teach the man a lesson so he will not be a menace to society in the future.

2. Since your legs are longer than your arms, you can be out of his reach and still strike him sharply

2

3

to the solar plexus with your heel by driving it
forward as though it were a left jab.

3. When the man falls down, don't let him get away.
Control his body by using a body pressure hold-
down on him.

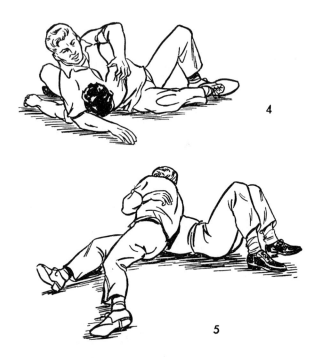

4

5

4. Take the slack out of his upper body by pulling his right sleeve and arm snug under your left shoulder. Place your right arm under his head or on the ground, leaning the right side of your body on his chest.

5. Spread your legs in an outrigger-tripod position. This will make it very difficult for your opponent to roll or get up. You should be able to hold him there until more help comes, or you can talk him out of any further action.

HE WHO DOES NOT THINK ABOUT
THE FUTURE MAY NOT HAVE ONE

1. I was walking down the street listening to the birds sing.
   All of a sudden a man jumped at me, he wanted a fling.

2. He grabbed me around the neck with a great deal of force.
   I could see he had done this before, without any remorse.

3. Here is a circle throw that looks like a wheel;
   The man I throw will go head over his heel.

4. With one leg on the ground and one on his belt,
   Nice and easy so it can hardly be felt.

5. I pull him in close until my back touches the ground.
   This man is wheeled over my leg, high and around.

6. I practice this throw in the gym day by day,
   So when destiny calls, even a king must obey.

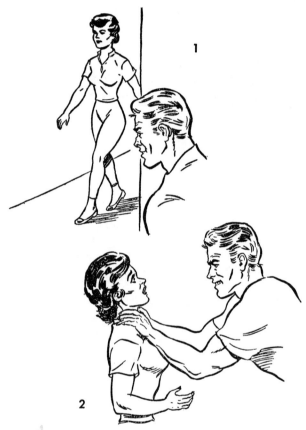

1. You can hold your head up high if you have confidence in the knowledge that if you get into a bad situation, you can handle it with ease.
2. If a man jumps at you and grabs you around the throat, do not get panicky. Calmly think of your next move.

3. Grab him by the lapels. Place your left foot below his belt and swing your right foot between his legs. This will get him to bend or lean forward.

4. After you roll on the ground, your opponent will fly over your body when you begin to straighten your left leg, raising him up at the waist and pulling his upper body close to you by bending your arms.

5. As you straighten your left leg, this will catapult his lower body high into the air.

6. He will fly over your body and land on the ground.

WHEN YOU ARE YOUNG, LEARN WISDOM AND WHEN YOU GET OLDER, PRACTICE IT

1. If a man's arms are longer than yours and he strikes at you with his fist,
   Put a club in your hand and you will be seven inches longer at the wrist.

2. One thing that really hurts is when you strike at his shins,
   But he will give it a second thought next time before he sins.

3. The club is a great advantage and will more than equalize.
   Hold the club with both hands, dance like you're striking at flies.

4. If he throws a left or a right, be very quick.
   When he lands, it will hurt him as he has hit your stick.

1. You will note that primarily a club is an extension
   to your arm. If you stand far enough away, your
   opponent can swing and miss, and if you have a
   seven- or ten-inch extension to your arm, naturally
   you can hit him without his hitting you.

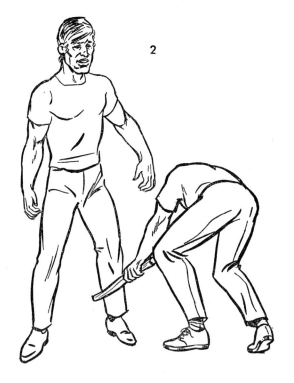

2

2. It is very difficult for anyone to counter any technique below his waist. You have very little flesh or protection over your shins. Strike between the knee and the ankle at the shins in front of the leg. Your opponent will find it very painful.

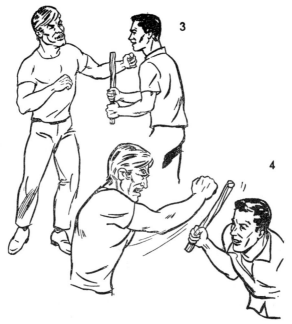

3. A man is in a boxer's position. Hold the club as though you were holding a baseball bat straight up and down. If the man swings his left, with a flick of your wrist only, knock his wrist or forearm with the striking part of the club. And if he throws a right, knock his right wrist or forearm, still keeping the club at the center of your body. Don't let the club get too far away from you. Do not reach. Let your opponent reach for you.

4. If your opponent is swinging a left or a right, hit his fist as though you were hitting a ball playing tennis. He will find it very painful. Keep your face and upper body out of his reach.

A FOOL LOOKS INTO A MAN'S EYES, A WISE MAN LOOKS INTO HIS HEART

1. If a man tries to part your hair with a baseball
   bat,
   Make your move fast before he knows where
   you are at.

2. Block his right with your left as he is winding
   it back.
   His arm will have no place to go; he can give
   you no crack.

3. Your right hand has his right arm in a very
   good hold.
   With your free hand, grab his bat; he won't
   feel so bold.

4. Put the bat in front of his neck, cross your arms
   in a scissoring motion,
   You can choke his neck by pushing your elbows
   forward, if you get the notion.

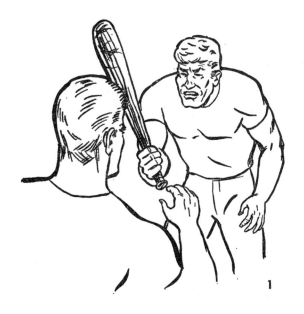

1. If a man tries to part your hair with a bat, move fast before it's too late.
2. When he swings at you with his right hand, first block with your left wrist at his wrist, putting his arm in a shoulder lock. Bring your right hand in back of his biceps and grip his wrist, securing the lock.
3. Then let go with your left hand, twisting the club out of his hand, still holding control of his body and arm with your right hand.

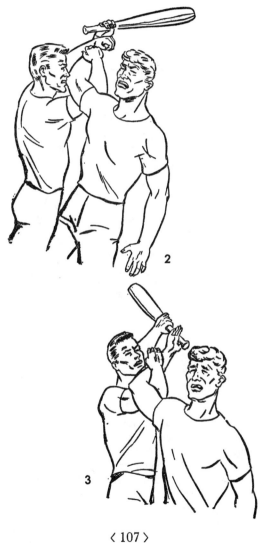

2

3

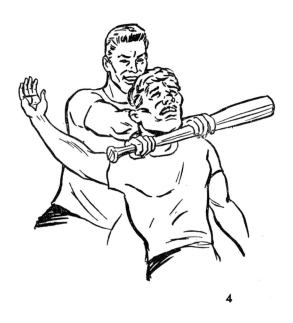

4

4. Using a cross-scissoring motion, slip the club
   around his neck, with your right hand on the left
   side of the club, your left hand on the right side
   of the club. His neck will be in the middle as if
   in a tourniquet. You can control him by applying
   pressure with a scissoring motion, dropping both
   elbows toward his shoulder.

⟨ 108 ⟩

ONE GOOD DEED IS BETTER THAN A THOUSAND GOOD INTENTIONS

1. He jumped over the fence, a little dog he would kick.
   He was bad news, so I picked up a stick.

2. I pulled his left sleeve to turn him around.
   There is no way I'd let him kick this little hound.

3. I pushed up at his collar to help me with this trick,
   And between his legs, with force I did shove my stick.

4. I turned my palm up, my come-along was his fate.
   No chance to kick this dog, as I walked him out the gate.

5. A good life does not depend on how many years it takes;
   But for sure how you spend them, for goodness sakes.

1. There is always the overgrown bully who takes advantage of a situation—in this example, by kicking at a small dog.

2. If this bully is a lot bigger than you, you must find an equalizer. If you pick up a thick stick or a club, this may do the trick. Grab the club in the middle with your right hand. With your left hand, swing your opponent so his back is toward you.

3. Switch your left hand to the back of his collar. Your right hand points the club between his legs.

2

3

〈 111 〉

4. When the club goes between his legs, twist it from left to right so that it is hooking the front part of his body, and you will have a handle. With this handle, you can walk the man in a come-along anywhere you desire. You will note that it is very difficult for a man to hit or kick you when you are behind him and he is off-balance leaning forward.

5. Do unto others as you would have others do unto you. Pet the dog and love him and he will love you in return.

A FOOL SHOWS AN OPEN KNIFE, A WISE MAN AN OPEN HAND

1. Don't take a chance with your life,
   If a man tries to stab you with his knife.

2. Quickly blind him by throwing dirt in his eyes.
   If he can't see, it will equalize your size.

3. Flex open the grip of his knife hand;
   Do this while he's still blinded by sand.

4. Important: keep his wrist flexed and don't be mild.
   Take his knife away like taking candy from a child.

5. Place the knife at his throat and hold his left limb.
   He won't move if he thinks you are serious with him.

1. Don't take any chances if a man tries to stab you with a knife.
2. Cut the odds down and put them in your favor by blinding him, throwing dirt or some handy object at his eyes.
3. When he is blinded, that is the time to attack, as he cannot see what direction you are coming from. Grab his wrist and flex it and bend it backward toward him, opening his hand.

⟨ 114 ⟩

2

3

〈115〉

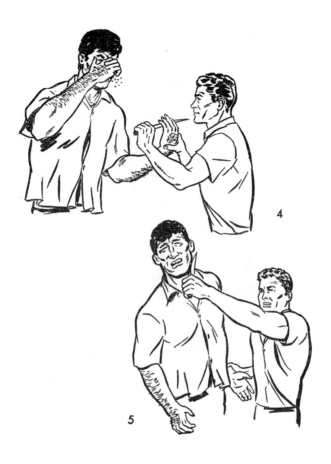

4. When his hand is open, strip the knife quickly out of his hand.
5. Place the knife at his neck and hold his left arm. If he moves, he will be the one to get hurt.

THE GREATEST GIFT IS TO SAVE A LIFE, AND MORE REWARDING IF IT'S YOUR OWN

1. Never attack a man with a knife,
   Because the danger will be to your life.

2. Let him stab at you, quickly parry at the wrist;
   His arm will fly up, your body he has missed.

3. Lean to your left and don't be tense,
   Attack his body, he will have no defense.

4. Balance your weight on one leg, your body is in
   a T position.
   Flip your foot at his body, that will finish your
   mission.

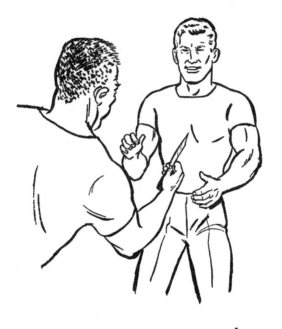

1

1. If a man has a knife, don't attack him. Let him attack you. In this way, he extends the knife away from his body.
2. At this point, parry the knife away from your body, striking at his wrist with your forearm.
3. Raise his arm up over his head, continuing your motion leaving the vulnerable parts of his body exposed.

2

3

4

4. Then, get into a **T** position, which means getting
   the vulnerable parts of your body, such as the neck,
   head, and stomach, far away from the knife. Thrust
   your leg out sharply, striking your shoe at his groin,
   solar plexus, or head, whichever is the quickest **and**
   easiest for you.

HE WHO WALKS AROUND IN A FOG WILL NEVER SEE THE LIGHT

1. A gun was placed in my back, hard enough to feel;
   It was my money this scoundrel wanted to steal.

2. I twisted to the left, my elbow knocked his gun aside.
   I had to do something, there was no place to hide.

3. I locked his gun wrist between my biceps and forearm with a smile,
   Because I knew now if the gun went off, it would miss me a mile.

4. I grabbed the gun, twisted it away before it could discharge.
   This man was big but without the gun, he was not so large.

5. Once I had his gun, this tiger became tame;
   He even turned into a pussycat when the police came.

1

1. If a man is directly behind you and puts a gun in your back, chances are if it is on the right side of your backbone, the gun will be in his right hand. If it is on the left side of your backbone, the gun will be in his left hand.

2. Turn sharply in the direction of the hand holding the gun, striking his forearm with your forearm, moving the gun away from your back.

3. Quickly wrap your arm around his wrist and grab the gun away from him with your free hand.

⟨ 122 ⟩

2

3

〈 123 〉

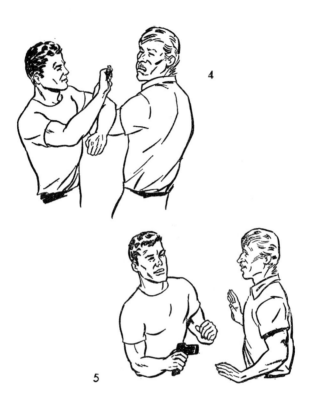

4. Still controlling his arm with your arm by keeping it close to your side, use your free hand to hold the gun-barrel and twist it toward his face. He will release the gun; you will end up with it.

5. When you end up with the gun, if you care to point it at him, make sure he is out of reach and not close enough to do anything until you have full control of the situation.

THE GOOD LORD GIVES YOU A MIND AND BODY; WHAT IS DONE WITH THEM IS UP TO YOU

1. With a gun know what you're doing before you
   get bold,
   Because if the gun goes off, you may never
   grow old.

2. Twisting, strike with the forearm the hand that
   holds the gun.
   If a bullet fires, it should miss your body and
   travel toward the sun.

3. Quickly grab the barrel and twist it toward
   his figure.
   If the gun is pointed toward him, he won't pull
   the trigger.

4. Keep twisting, he'll let go of the gun without
   taking a fall.
   Now you have the gun and this time the villain
   takes no haul.

1. You may assume that any time a man sticks a gun in your stomach, he is liable to use it, so raise your hands over your head and keep your elbows very close to your side.

2. Turn your body quickly from right to left by using your forearm against your opponent's wrist. If the gun fires at this point, it should miss your body.

3. With your left hand, quickly grab your opponent's gun and bend it toward his stomach, flexing and bending his wrist. His wrist will then automatically open and he will lose his grip on the gun.

2

3

4

4. Take the gun out of his hand quickly and step **back** out of his reach.

⟨ 128 ⟩

ABOUT THE AUTHOR

GENE LEBELL is a recognized authority on judo and self-defense, both as a published author and licensed teacher. He operates his own *dojo* in Los Angeles, which teaches judo, karate, and self-defense, and is himself a 5th-degree black-belt holder in Kodokan Judo.

Mr. LeBell has wrestled professionally all over the world and has also appeared in most of the major U.S. TV shows and motion pictures, as stuntman/actor. For the past few years, Gene has been a successful sports announcer on local TV stations. He is also the author of two books, "Handbook of Judo" and "Handbook of Self-Defense."

(Circa 1971)

ABOUT THE BOOK

HERE AT LAST is a useful little illustrated guide to self-defense that everyone can and should afford! It outlines thirty probable circumstances in which a man or woman could be confronted with an attack by an assailant and it tells and shows how to survive such attacks.

A unique self-teacher in itself, it stimulates further study by the addition of poetic verse for each of the 138 line drawings, as supplements to the regular instructions. The author makes it plain to the reader, however, that "the rules of fair play were thrown out the window because this is a deadly serious little book designed to save you from a bad beating, or worse."